The Tiara Club

at Diamond Turrets

6–10
5–

For Lindsey, with love and hugs xxx
VF
With very special thanks to JD

www.tiaraclub.co.uk

ORCHARD BOOKS
338 Euston Road, London NW1 3BH
Orchard Books Australia
Level 17/207 Kent St, Sydney, NSW 2000

A Paperback Original
First published in Great Britain in 2009
Text copyright © Vivian French 2009
Cover illustration copyright © Sarah Gibb 2009
Inside illustrations copyright © Orchard Books 2009

The right of Vivian French to be identified as the author of this
work has been asserted by her in accordance with the Copyright,
Designs and Patents Act 1988.

A CIP catalogue record for this book is available
from the British Library.

ISBN 978 1 84616 878 9

1 3 5 7 9 10 8 6 4 2

Printed in Great Britain

Orchard Books is a division of Hachette Children's Books,
an Hachette UK company

www.hachette.co.uk

The Tiara Club

at Diamond Turrets

Princess Lindsey

and the Fluffy Guinea Pig

By Vivian French

ORCHARD BOOKS

The Royal Palace Academy
for the Preparation of Perfect Princesses

(Known to our students as "*The Princess Academy*")

OUR SCHOOL MOTTO:
A Perfect Princess always thinks of others
before herself, and is kind, caring and truthful.

Diamond Turrets offers a complete education for Tiara Club princesses, focusing on caring for animals and the environment. The curriculum includes:

A visit to the Royal County Show	*Visits to the Country Park and Bamboo Grove*
Work experience on our very own farm	*Elephant rides in our Safari Park (students will be closely supervised)*

Our headteacher, King Percy, is present at all times, and students are well looked after by Fairy G, the school Fairy Godmother.

Our resident staff and visiting experts include:

LADY WHITSTABLE KENT
(IN CHARGE OF THE FARM,
COUNTRY PARK AND SAFARI PARK)

FAIRY ANGORA
(ASSISTANT FAIRY GODMOTHER)

QUEEN MOTHER MATILDA
(ETIQUETTE, POSTURE AND
APPEARANCE)

FARMER KATE
(DOMESTIC ANIMALS)

LADY MAY (SUPERVISOR OF THE
HOLIDAY HOME FOR PETS)

We award tiara points to encourage our Tiara Club princesses towards the next level. All princesses who win enough points at Diamond Turrets will be presented with their Diamond Sashes and attend a celebration ball.

Diamond Sash Tiara Club princesses are invited to return to Golden Gates, our magnificent mansion residence for Perfect Princesses, where they may continue their education at a higher level.

PLEASE NOTE:
Princesses are expected to arrive at the Academy with a *minimum* of:

TWENTY BALLGOWNS
(with all necessary hoops, petticoats, etc)

TWELVE DAY DRESSES

SEVEN GOWNS
suitable for garden parties and other special day occasions

TWELVE TIARAS

DANCING SHOES
five pairs

VELVET SLIPPERS
three pairs

RIDING BOOTS
two pairs

Wellington boots, waterproof cloaks and other essential protective clothing as required

Dear Princess – I'm
SO pleased to meet you!
I'm Princess Lindsey, and maybe you've
already met Mia, Bethany, Caitlin, Abigail
and Rebecca? We all share Tulip Room,
and we're the very best friends ever.
Do you have a pet? There's a fabulous
Holiday Home for Pets here at Diamond
Turrets, and we all help look after
the animals that come to stay – it's
SUCH fun...except when the twins
cause trouble, of course!

Chapter One

My most favourite animals are guinea pigs – I just LOVE them! Their eyes are just a little bit too close together, which makes them look really sweet, and they make the cutest *wink! wink!* noise.

When I arrived at Diamond Turrets and discovered there was a Holiday Home for Pets as well as the farm and the safari park I was SO thrilled. The first thing I asked was, "Are there any guinea pigs staying at the moment?" and I was really disappointed when there weren't. But then, one Thursday, it was Tulip Room's turn to work with the pets – and there was the most DIVINE guinea pig. He was trying to hide himself under a lettuce leaf, but his bottom was sticking out. (That's another of the reasons why I love guinea pigs so much; they're just SO silly.)

"Wow," I breathed. "Where did he come from?"

Lady May, who looks after the Holiday Home, smiled at me. "He belongs to Diamonde and Gruella's aunt, and their cousins. I'm worried about him, though. He arrived yesterday evening, and he hasn't eaten anything."

"Maybe he was upset by the journey," Abigail suggested.

Lady May looked doubtful. "Most guinea pigs can't resist cucumber, or carrot. But I've tried him with just about everything, and he isn't interested."

"Could I try?" I asked, but before Lady May could answer, Diamonde and Gruella sailed through the door.

"Where's Monty?" Diamonde demanded. "Auntie Emmalina said he was coming to stay here while she's on tour, and WE want to look after him!" And she and Gruella pushed their way in front of us until they were leaning over the top of Monty's cage.

"Hello, Monty," Gruella said loudly. She made a grab at him, but he squeaked wildly and ran behind his water bottle.

"Oh – please don't scare him!"
I burst out. I couldn't help myself;
Monty was trembling all over.
Gruella and Diamonde glared
at me.

"He belongs to OUR cousins,"
Diamonde told me fiercely. "He's
nothing to do with you. Look – he
knows ME!"

Lady May made a tut-tutting noise as Monty scuttled away from Diamonde's clutching hands. "I think we should leave him alone until he's settled down," she said. "Why don't you come and help me feed the rabbits?"

Diamonde gave me a suspicious glance. "Is Lindsey going to come too?"

"Of course I am," I said, and I wheeled myself over to the rabbits' hutches. Both the twins followed me, and I saw Bethany give me a tiny thumbs up. Caitlin and Rebecca had been cleaning out the run, and as they went to

wash their hands Lady May asked
Mia to fetch the basket of carrots.
Abigail handed us each a bunch
of lettuce leaves, and Diamonde
screamed.

"YUCK! There's a horrible
SLUG!" She dropped her leaves

on the floor, and ran towards the sink. She shoved Caitlin and Rebecca to one side, and turned on the tap so hard that water splashed everywhere. "I HATE slugs!" she wailed. "I just HATE them! They're so..."

"Slimy?" I suggested, and I really, REALLY didn't meant to smile, but I did.

Diamonde looked absolutely furious. "Are you laughing at me, Princess Lindsey?" she asked. "Because you'll be VERY sorry if you are!" She threw the towel down, and flounced off. Gruella hesitated, then went after her.

Chapter Two

"Oh dear." Lady May looked upset. "I don't think that's quite the right way for a Perfect Princess to behave. Perhaps I should give Diamonde a minus tiara point? But slugs are really rather horrid, aren't they?"

We weren't quite sure what to say. Lady May is very nice, but she's so kind, she lets the twins do more or less what they want. I wheeled myself back to have a look at Monty, and I saw he was still hiding behind his water bottle.

"Hey, Monty!" I whispered. "Hey! Do you want a bit of lettuce?" I poked a little leaf through the bars while I went on talking to him. His ears twitched, and then – very slowly, and keeping his little black eyes fixed on my face – he came to the bars and took the leaf. He ate it as if he was starving, and before very long he'd eaten everything I had on my lap.

"Well done, Lindsey." Lady May

was standing just behind me. "See if you can get him to eat some dry food."

I nodded, and took the handful of seeds she gave me. Monty wouldn't eat anything if I put it on the floor of his cage, but he ate everything I gave him by hand. And then he nuzzled against my fingers, and pushed at them to make me tickle him behind his ears.

Five minutes later he was sitting on my lap, chuntering happily away to himself while I stroked his fur and made a fuss of him.

"Can I hold him?" Abigail asked me.

"Give him a tickle first," I said, but when she did, Monty let out a loud protesting squeak and tried to hide under my arm.

Lady May shook her head. "He knows who he likes. You'd better come back this evening to feed him, Princess Lindsey. He's here until Saturday, and we don't want him to go home looking skinny."

"I'd love to." Very gently I put Monty back in his cage, and he skipped off to doze in a corner. I waved him goodbye, and went to join my friends. There was a little black and white collie dog called Minnie who had come to stay, and they were about to take her for a walk. Lady May told us to be sure we got her back in time for us to have lunch, and we promised we would.

"Oh – and Princess Lindsey! I'll give you five tiara points for your excellent work this morning," she said as we set off, Minnie bounding happily beside us.

"Wow!" Caitlin patted me on the back. "Five tiara points for being kind to a guinea pig! That'll show the twins what they're missing."

"WHAT are we missing?" Diamonde appeared as if by magic

from behind a bush, Gruella beside her.

Abigail jumped. "Whatever are you doing there, Diamonde?"

Diamonde didn't answer. She pointed at Caitlin. "What are we missing?"

Caitlin sighed. "Lady May gave Lindsey five tiara points, if you must know."

"What for?" Gruella's nose was almost quivering. "She didn't give US any tiara points, did she, Diamonde? And you had a HORRIBLE fright with that slimy slug."

Diamonde nodded. "That's right. So how come Lindsey got points?"

"She persuaded Monty to eat his dinner," Abigail told her. "And now, if you'll excuse us, we need to get on with our walk—"

"Just a minute!" Diamonde

grabbed the handles of my wheelchair. "That's OUR guinea pig! You leave him alone!"

Do you know something? I really hate it when people grab my chair. It makes me cross, and that sometimes makes me say things I shouldn't. Usually I do my very best to ignore the twins when they're being silly, but this time I didn't. "Actually, Lady May wants me to feed him this evening," I snapped. I pulled myself away from them, and zoomed off down the path – and I didn't look back.

Chapter Three

By the time my friends had caught up with me, I'd cooled down. Bethany told me the twins had hurried off muttering, but I didn't mind. I was already looking forward to seeing Monty again at the end of the day.

We took Minnie for a good long walk, and got back to school just in time to wash our hands for lunch. Our fairy godmother, Fairy G, was sitting next to Lady May in the dining hall, and as we were finishing our pudding she came bustling towards us.

"Well done, Tulip Room!" she boomed. "Lady May tells me you're a guinea pig wizard, Lindsey. And she's delighted with the way you all worked today; she's asked me to give you three tiara points each." Fairy G stopped, and gave Diamonde and Gruella a rather cool look. "I hear you made a fuss about a slug, Diamonde. If you're going to work with animals I'm afraid that's part of the experience. A Perfect Princess must rise above such things."

Diamonde shrugged, and stared at the table. Fairy G stomped off to talk to Daffodil Room, and my friends and I began to chat about what we were going to do at the weekend. There weren't any parties or balls or picnics, so Rebecca suggested that maybe we could spend Saturday helping in the Pets' Holiday Home, as it was SO much fun.

There was a loud snort from behind us, and I saw Diamonde giving me her snootiest look.

"You needn't think you can play with Monty," she told me. "Auntie Emmalina's coming to collect him on Saturday, so he'll be gone by lunchtime. And Gruella and I are going back with Auntie for a very special dancing party in the evening, and nobody else from here is invited!"

"I hope you have a nice time," Mia said politely. "And I'm sure Monty will be delighted to be home again."

Diamonde snorted again. "He'll be pleased to get away from Lindsey." She picked up her plate. "Come on, Gruella. We've got better things to do than stand here talking to the silly Tulips!"

Gruella was bending down and peering at something under our table, but she stood up and marched off with her sister.

"Is it very unprincessy to say we'll be pleased the twins won't be here on Saturday?" Bethany asked as we watched them flounce out of the dining hall.

Caitlin giggled. "Probably," she said. "But I do agree."

"Why don't we take Minnie for an extra special walk on Saturday?" Rebecca suggested.

Abigail shook her head. "Lady May said she was going to take her out. But I suppose we could go with her."

That didn't sound quite as exciting as going on our own, so we decided to wait and see.

As we were going out of the hall we met the twins coming back, and they were both smiling in the strangest way.

Gruella saw us looking, and blushed bright pink. "We...er, we forgot something," she said, and scuttled past as fast as she could.

I was certain they were up to some kind of mischief, and I turned to watch. Diamonde walked straight to the table where we'd been sitting, and dived underneath it while Gruella held up the tablecloth. I was just about to tell the others when...

Clang! Clang! Clang! The bell rang for afternoon school. By the time we'd finished "Choosing Books for a Royal Library", I'd forgotten all about them.

Chapter Four

As the bell sounded for the end of school I suddenly noticed my bracelet was missing. "Bother," I said, and I asked Rebecca if she'd seen it anywhere. She said she hadn't, and I wondered if I'd forgotten to put it on that morning. I left the others doing their homework and went to look in Tulip Room, but it wasn't beside my bed where I keep it when I'm not wearing it. I thought of going to ask Fairy G if it was in the lost property basket, but I REALLY wanted to see Monty again, so I didn't. Caitlin and Mia said they'd come with me, and after we'd done our homework in record time we made our way out of school.

There was no one in the Holiday Home when we arrived, so I wheeled myself straight up to Monty's cage...and he was gone!

"Oh NO!" I looked all round the floor, and in all the other cages,

but there was no sign of him.
"Monty!" I called. "Monty!"

Caitlin and Mia rushed to look
in the hay bin, and the food store,
but he wasn't there either.

"We'd better tell Lady May," I said, but at that moment the door opened and Lady May came hurrying in. She was closely followed by the twins, who were both crying, but I was almost certain they were putting it on because I couldn't see any sign of real tears.

"Princess Lindsey!" Lady May gave me SUCH a stern look. "The twins tell me you have taken Monty out of his cage without my permission! Where have you put him?"

I could feel my mouth falling open as I stared at her. "But I haven't touched him!" I said.

Diamonde scowled at me. "We know it was you. He doesn't let anyone else pick him up, does he?"

My stomach suddenly felt as if it was doing cartwheels, because I knew she was right. Then Gruella gave a loud squeal. "Look! What's that?" She fished about in the hay, and I saw something shining...and she held up my bracelet.

Lady May looked even sterner. "Is that yours, Princess Lindsey?"

I nodded, and my mind was whirling. Diamonde had stopped crying and was looking incredibly pleased with herself – and I was as certain as could be that she wasn't surprised my bracelet was in the cage.

"Well, Princess Lindsey? What have you got to say for yourself?" Lady May sounded angrier than I'd ever heard her sound before.

I sat up very straight, and took a deep breath. "I PROMISE I didn't take Monty out of his cage," I said, as clearly and as seriously as I could.

"You DID! You're a kidnapper!" Diamonde's voice was very shrill.

Mia put her hand up. "Excuse me, Lady May, but we've been with Lindsey ever since school ended. She couldn't have...at least..." She stopped dead, and I knew she'd remembered I'd left the homework room.

"See?" Gruella was jubilant. "Lindsey DID do it! She's hidden Monty away!"

Lady May was looking puzzled. She turned to Mia. "Did you say you'd been with Lindsey all afternoon?"

Mia swallowed, and I said quickly, "I did leave the homework room to look for my bracelet, but I was only gone a few minutes." I wheeled round to ask Caitlin if she agreed, and to my amazement she wasn't there. My stomach gave another lurch. Had she slipped away because she thought I'd done something horrible?

Lady May sighed. "I think we'd better take this to Fairy G. The most important thing right now is to find that poor little guinea pig. Wherever he is, he must be feeling very frightened. Please come with me, Princess Lindsey."

Chapter Five

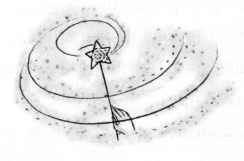

"We'll come too," Diamonde said as Lady May got up and began walking to the door. "It's our auntie's pet, and we KNOW Lindsey took it."

"And HOW do you know Lindsey took it?" boomed a loud voice. We all jumped, even Lady May. Fairy G was standing right in the middle of the Pets' Holiday Home, and not one of us had seen her come in...and Caitlin was there too. She gave me little secret smile, and I realised she'd run to fetch help.

Diamonde folded her arms.

"Nobody can pick Monty up except Lindsey," she told Fairy G. "AND her bracelet was in the hay in Monty's cage!"

Fairy G raised an eyebrow. "I see." She waved her wand, and showers of twinkly stars whirled round and round. Minnie began to bark, and Fairy G began to chuckle. "There's our answer," she said. "We'll ask Minnie to find Monty for us. Caitlin, dear, would you fetch her, please?"

As Caitlin hurried to put Minnie on her lead, Diamonde whispered in Gruella's ear. Gruella looked anxious. "Diamonde says Monty's absolutely terrified of dogs," she told Fairy G. "Minnie might catch him and eat him!"

"Not while I'm here," Fairy G said firmly. "Now, let's get going!" And before we knew what was happening, the twins, Mia and I were outside with Caitlin and Minnie. Minnie's ears were twitching, and Fairy G tapped her on the head very lightly with her wand. "Find Monty, Minnie!" she ordered, and Minnie gave a short sharp bark as if she was saying, "Yes!"

"Erm...erm..." Diamonde was fidgeting madly. "Erm...I think

I might let you find Monty on your own, Fairy G. Gruella and I have to go and sort something out—"

"You will stay with us, Diamonde." Fairy G began to grow, so I knew she was getting angry, and Diamonde went pale.

"Yes, Fairy G," she muttered, and she and Gruella trailed beside us as Minnie led us away from the Holiday Home, and back towards school. In through the side door she went, and along the corridor... all the way to the twins' room.

Minnie stopped outside, and Fairy G looked at Diamonde and Gruella.

"Have you anything to say?" she asked. They both shook their heads, and Fairy G opened the door.

At first we couldn't see anything unusual, but the next minute there was a loud *Wink! Wink! Wink!* and Monty rushed out from underneath Diamonde's bed. He came scuttling towards me as fast as his little legs would carry him, and Fairy G gave a little *flip!* with her wand – and there he was on my lap, snuggling down.

Diamonde let out a piercing shriek. "OH!!! Lindsey must have put him in our room! How COULD you, Lindsey?"

Fairy G looked at us all. "Now," she said, "who's going to tell me the truth?"

There was a long pause.

Fairy G gave Diamonde one of her most piercing stares. "Did you say you and Gruella couldn't pick Monty up, Diamonde?"

Diamonde nodded. "He just runs away from us. You can ask Lady May – she saw him!"

"But perhaps the two of you could have caught him together?"

Diamonde looked at Fairy G like a frightened rabbit, but she still shook her head. Fairy G sighed, and waved her wand. There was a strange fizzing noise, and I saw tiny golden sparkles twinkling all over Diamonde and Gruella's hands and dresses. I looked down, and Monty was twinkling all over too. I gave him a little stroke, and a flurry of sparkles flew off my fingers.

Gruella put her hand to her mouth. "We should have washed and changed our clothes, Diamonde!" she whispered. "We're COVERED in guinea pig fur!"

Chapter Six

Diamonde tried to make out that she'd only hidden Monty away to tease me, but that just made Fairy G even crosser. The twins were sent to King Percy, our headteacher, and he told them that they would most certainly NOT be allowed to go out with their aunt when she came to collect Monty.

Rebecca said she thought our headteacher was especially angry because Diamonde had hidden my bracelet in the hay, and I think she might have been right. Anyway, the twins were very quiet all the next day, and when Saturday came they wouldn't come out of their room.

We hurried down to the Pets' Holiday Home, and when we got there we had SUCH a surprise! There was a queen and three little princes in Lady May's office, and the littlest prince had Monty on his knee.

When we came in, Lady May

stepped forward to introduce us. "This is Queen Emmalina," she said. "She wanted to thank you, Lindsey, for looking after Monty so well."

Queen Emmalina beamed at me.

"You were SO clever to make him eat," she said. "He is EXTREMELY fussy, I'm afraid. I'd love to thank you properly. Perhaps you and your friends would like to come back with me and the boys for our party tonight?"

We looked at each other in

astonishment. "That would be BRILLIANT," I said. "But...but what about the twins? It doesn't seem fair that we should come, when they can't." A sudden thought came to me, and I took a deep breath. "Please...would you excuse me for a moment?"

And I twirled my wheelchair round and headed for the school.

It took me two minutes to find King Percy, but about another ten to convince him that I MIGHT just have lost my bracelet in the hay. In the end he called Fairy G into his study.

"What do you think, Fairy G?" he asked. "Should we allow the twins their treat?"

Fairy G's eyes began to twinkle. "'A Perfect Princess always forgives her enemies,'" she quoted. "And I won't mention the fact that I MIGHT have seen Lindsey's bracelet under the dining room table. It will do the twins good to know that there are such kind and generous princesses here at Diamond Turrets."

*

So...the twins were allowed to come with us. They didn't do

much dancing at the party, but they were VERY nice to us, and we had the most FABULOUS time.

They kept thanking me, and when we got back to Diamond Turrets the next day I found a note on my bed.

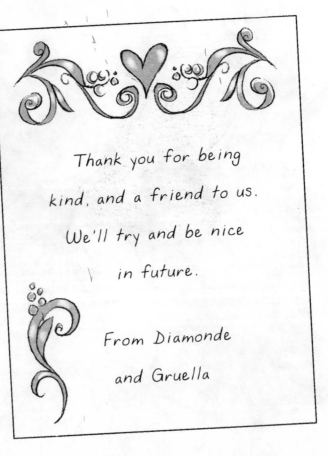

Thank you for being kind, and a friend to us. We'll try and be nice in future.

From Diamonde and Gruella

But the twins will never be as wonderful a friend as you...

Because you're the very best friend EVER!

Don't miss  *The* **Tiara** *Club* website at:

www.tiaraclub.co.uk

Keep up to date with the latest
Tiara Club books and meet all
your favourite princesses!

There is SO much to see and do,
including games and activities. You can
even become an exclusive member of the
Tiara Club Princess Academy.

PLUS, there are exciting
competitions with truly
FABULOUS prizes!

Be a Perfect Princess – check it out today!

What happens next?
Find out in

Princess Abigail
and the Baby Panda

Hello! My name's Abigail - what's yours?
And isn't it fun being
here at Diamond Turrets?
I absolutely LOVE it, even though the
twins can be really horrible sometimes.
I don't mind, though. I've got lovely Mia,
Bethany, Caitlin, Lindsey and Rebecca
to keep me company - and you're
here too, which is wonderful!

Do you have morning assemblies at your school? We have them three times a week at Diamond Turrets, and they're really exciting. Sometimes King Percy, our head teacher, tells us how all the different animals are getting on, and sometimes Lady Whitstable-Kent has a new project for us. Lady Whit's in charge of the country park, the farm and the animals, and she can be just a little bit terrifying. Lindsey says she's very nice and kind when you get to know her, but I'm not sure I really want to try.

Anyway, it was Lady Whit's turn to take assembly, and she came to the front of the platform with a HUGE smile on her face.

"Dear princesses," she began, "I have some wonderful news for you. King Percy and I have been keeping a very special secret for three whole months, but now at last we can tell you...

~ Want to read more? ~
Princess Abigail and the Baby Panda
is out now!